The Kentucky Wildcats ®

BY

MARK STEWART

Content Consultant
Matt Zeysing
Historian and Archivist
The Naismith Memorial Basketball Hall of Fame

NORWOODHOUSE 🏠 PRESS
CHICAGO, ILLINOIS

Norwood House Press
P.O. Box 316598
Chicago, Illinois 60631

For information regarding Norwood House Press, please visit our website at:
www.norwoodhousepress.com or call 866-565-2900.

All photos courtesy of Getty Images except the following:
Associated Press (5, 8, 19, 24, 29, 31, 33, 40), Collegiate Collection (6, 41 top right),
Press Pass, Inc. (7), Foodtown Supermarkets of Kentucky, Inc. (9, 37 top left, 39),
University of Kentucky (21, 41 bottom left & right), Sports Legends (14), Dell Publishing (16),
Editions Rencontre, S.A. (18), Macfadden Publications, Inc. (22), Pacific Trading Cards, Inc. (23),
Icon SMI (25), Sports Review Publishing Co. (36), Matt Richman (48).
Cover Photo: Andy Lyons/Getty Images

Special thanks to Topps, Inc.

Editor: Mike Kennedy
Designer: Ron Jaffe
Project Management: Black Book Partners, LLC.
Editorial Production: Jessica McCulloch
Research: Joshua Zaffos
Thanks to Teddy Dahlman and Nick Phelps

Library of Congress Cataloging-in-Publication Data

Stewart, Mark, 1960-
  The Kentucky Wildcats / by Mark Stewart.
     p. cm. -- (Team spirit--college basketball)
  Includes bibliographical references and index.
  Summary: "Presents the history and accomplishments of the University of
Kentucky Wildcats basketball team. Includes highlights of players, coaches,
and awards, longstanding rivalries, quotes, timeline, maps, glossary, and
websites"--Provided by publisher.
  ISBN-13: 978-1-59953-367-4 (library edition : alk. paper)
  ISBN-10: 1-59953-367-7 (library edition : alk. paper)
  1. University of Kentucky--Basketball--History--Juvenile literature. 2.
Kentucky Wildcats (Basketball team)--History--Juvenile literature. I.
Title.
  GV885.43.U53S74 2010
  796.323'630976947--dc22
                                                      2009033810

Manufactured in the United States of America in North Mankato, Minnesota.
159N—072010

COVER PHOTO: Kentucky's mascots and cheerleaders show their team spirit during the 2004–05 season.

Table of Contents

CHAPTER	PAGE
Meet the Wildcats	4
Way Back When	6
21st Century	10
Home Court	12
Dressed for Success	14
We're Number 1!	16
Go-To Guys: Trophy Case	20
Go-To Guys: Super Scorers	22
Go-To Guys: Game Changers	24
On the Sidelines	26
Rivals	28
One Great Day	30
It Really Happened	32
Team Spirit	34
Timeline	36
Fun Facts	38
For the Record	40
The SEC	42
The College Game	44
Glossary	46
Places to Go	47
Index	48

SPORTS WORDS & VOCABULARY WORDS: In this book, you will find many words that are new to you. You may also see familiar words used in new ways. The glossary on page 46 gives the meanings of basketball words, as well as "everyday" words that have special basketball meanings. These words appear in **bold type** throughout the book. The glossary on page 47 gives the meanings of vocabulary words that are not related to basketball. They appear in ***bold italic type*** throughout the book.

Meet the Wildcats

Basketball was not invented in Kentucky. However, according to many fans of the University of Kentucky, that is where the game was perfected! They may have a point. Since the 1940s, few college sports programs can match the team's year-in, year-out success. And no **professional** team in the state has ever been able to compete with the Wildcats for the hearts of Kentucky sports fans.

Over the years, the school has won the **National Collegiate Athletic Association (NCAA)** championship seven times. Since joining the **Southeastern Conference (SEC)** in 1932, the Wildcats have won more than 40 league titles. It is an amazing record of success.

This book tells the story of the Wildcats. Many of basketball's finest players have worn the blue and white. Some of the game's greatest coaches have called the school's Lexington *campus* "home." Along with Kentucky's students and fans, they are part of a big blue nation that numbers in the millions and stretches across the globe.

Anthony Epps, Antoine Walker, and Ron Mercer celebrate during Kentucky's run to the 1996 national championship.

Way Back When

KENTUCKY'S
FINEST

ADOLPH
RUPP

Basketball was America's most popular new sport in the early 1900s. But while many people played the game, few colleges had actually started teams. Kentucky was one of the first schools to embrace the sport.

In 1902, basketball was first played on campus by young women. The following year, a group of young men raised $3 to buy a basketball and then formed a team. They played three games that season and lost twice. In 1912, the Wildcats enjoyed their first undefeated season. In 1921, coach George Buchheit and **All-American** Basil Hayden led Kentucky to the league championship.

In 1930, the school hired Adolph Rupp to coach the team. By his third year, the Wildcats were the country's top squad. Rupp trained his players to win with *suffocating* defense and a fast-moving offense. An opponent had to be in top condition to beat Kentucky.

Rupp coached the Wildcats for 42 years. During that time, they won 27 SEC titles and also won the conference tournament 13 times. They were national champions in 1948, 1949, 1951, and 1958.

Among Rupp's many stars were several all-time great players. During the 1940s, the Wildcats were led by Ralph Beard and Alex Groza. During the 1950s, their top players included Adrian Smith, Cliff Hagan, Frank Ramsey, Jerry Bird, and Johnny Cox. Rupp's teams in the 1960s and early 1970s featured Charles "Cotton" Nash, Pat Riley, Louie Dampier, and Dan Issel. These players were very good when they arrived at Kentucky. Rupp drove them to excellence during their years with the Wildcats.

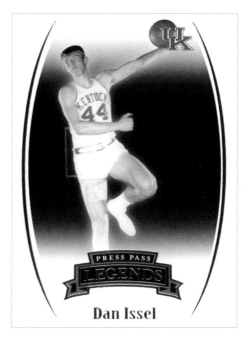

Dan Issel

In 1972, Rupp retired and his assistant, Joe B. Hall, took over. Hall also **recruited** many talented players, including Kevin Grevey, Rick Robey, Kyle Macy, and Jack Givens. He guided the Wildcats to the NCAA championship game in 1975. In 1978, Kentucky won the national title for the fifth time.

LEFT: Adolph Rupp, the most successful coach in Kentucky history.
ABOVE: Dan Issel, one of Rupp's greatest players.

During the 1980s, Kentucky often struggled to win as consistently as it had in previous *eras*. Sam Bowie, Mel Turpin, Kenny Walker, and Rex Chapman were great players, but they could not change the school's fortunes. The Wildcats turned things around after hiring Rick Pitino to coach the squad in 1989.

Pitino brought a fast-paced style of basketball back to Kentucky. He won the national championship in 1996 with a team that starred Antoine Walker, Tony Delk, Ron Mercer, and Walter McCarty. In all, nine players from that squad went on to play in the **National Basketball Association (NBA)**.

Cat Card #11

Freshman Center
1979-1980
Kentucky Wildcat

Pitino also decided to move on to the NBA. But his former assistant, Orlando "Tubby" Smith, picked up right where he left off. He relied heavily on Wayne Turner, a quick and tough guard who had played for the 1996 champs. In 1998, the Wildcats won the national championship again—their seventh in 51 seasons. The school's *tradition* of excellent basketball continued.

LEFT: Ron Mercer rises for a jump shot in the 1996 championship game.
ABOVE: A trading card of Sam Bowie.

21st Century

The recipe for basketball success at Kentucky hasn't changed in 80 years. The coach's job is to build a team around the talent and strengths of his players, and then push them to achieve great things. In most years, this means out-running and out-shooting opponents. But under coach Tubby Smith, the Wildcats were at their best when they slowed the game down. They learned to win with good defense and rebounding. Fans nicknamed this style of play "Tubby-Ball."

The Wildcats used this *strategy* to win five SEC championships from 1998 to 2004. Their stars during this period included Tayshaun Prince, Jamaal Magloire, Keith Bogans, Kelenna Azubuike, and Rajon Rondo. After Smith left the team in 2007, Kentucky continued to put top players on the court, including Randolph Morris and Jodie Meeks.

As the Wildcats head into a new era, their fans expect big things. They want more than a conference championship or the top **seed** in the **NCAA Tournament**. Kentucky has built a tradition of basketball excellence. Fans of the Wildcats want another national championship.

The Wildcats show which team is #1 after winning the SEC Tournament in 2003.

Home Court

The Wildcats play their home games in Rupp Arena. It was the largest basketball stadium in the United States when it was built in 1976. Rupp Arena is part of a popular shopping and tourism neighborhood in downtown Lexington.

The arena is named after beloved coach Adolph Rupp. It was completed a year before he died. While Rupp was coaching, the Wildcats played in Alumni Gymnasium and Memorial Coliseum.

Rupp Arena is one of the noisiest in college basketball. Not only does it have more seats than just about any other college arena, it also has a standing-room section called the eRUPPtion Zone. The students who squeeze into this section make sure it lives up to its name.

BY THE NUMBERS

- *There are 23,500 seats for basketball in Rupp Arena.*
- *The arena cost $53 million to build in 1976.*
- *In 2008, the university announced that it planned to build a new stadium sometime in the future. It will hold up to 30,000 fans.*

Fans fill Rupp Arena for a game in 2005. Banners celebrating Kentucky's best seasons hang from the ceiling.

Dressed for Success

Kentucky's uniform has used blue and white since the first time the school put a team on the court. In fact, the school made these colors official in 1892—more than a **decade** before the first basketball game was played. The players wear white uniforms with blue numbers at home and blue uniforms with white numbers on the road.

Kentucky's **logo** has almost always included the letters *UK*. For a time, it showed the outline of the state with the head of a wildcat, or bobcat. In 1989, the school added a **ferocious** wildcat to its traditional *UK* logo.

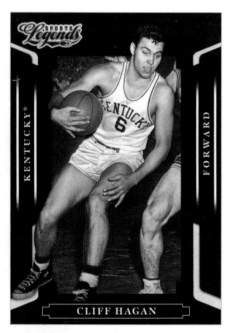

For one season in the 1990s, the Wildcats wore denim uniforms. In 2008, Kentucky switched to a new uniform design. The uniforms were made to look like the ones Team USA wore at that year's **Olympics**. The blue road uniform has squares like the racing silks worn by jockeys. This reminds fans of one of the state's other favorite sports, horse racing.

A trading card shows Cliff Hagan in the Kentucky uniform from the 1950s.

UNIFORM BASICS

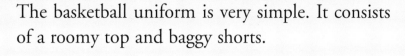

The basketball uniform is very simple. It consists of a roomy top and baggy shorts.

- The top hangs from the shoulders, with big "scoops" for the arms and neck. This style has not changed much over the years.

- Shorts, however, have changed a lot. They used to be very short, so players could move their legs freely. In the last 20 years, shorts have gotten longer and much baggier.

Basketball uniforms look the same as they did long ago … until you look very closely. In the old days, the shorts had belts and buckles. The tops were made of a thick cotton called "jersey," which got very heavy when players sweated. Later, uniforms were made of shiny *satin*. They may have looked great, but they did not "breathe." As a result, players got very hot! Today, most uniforms are made of ***synthetic*** materials that soak up sweat and keep the body cool.

Jodie Meeks wears the uniform that the Wildcats introduced in 2008.

We're Number 1!

During the 1940s and 1950s, no team in college basketball was better than Kentucky. The Wildcats won more games during those decades than any other college team. They also claimed one **National Invitation Tournament (NIT)** championship and four NCAA championships.

The core of the team in the 1940s was the "Fabulous Five"—Alex Groza, Ralph Beard, Wallace "Wah Wah" Jones, Cliff Barker, and Kenny Rollins. Beard and Jones were the stars in 1945–46, when Kentucky defeated Rhode Island in the NIT title game, 46–45. Beard did a great job guarding superstar Ernie Calverley. He also made the winning free throw with 40 seconds left.

In 1948, all five stars were in the **lineup** when Kentucky won the NCAA title. Barker, the only senior, showed why he was the team's defensive leader. In the semifinal battle with Holy Cross, he held lightning-

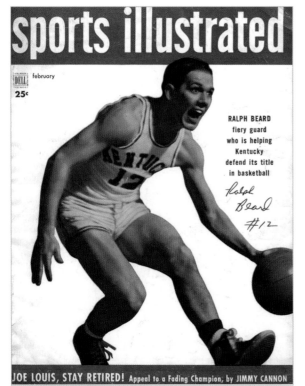

sports illustrated

february

25¢

RALPH BEARD
fiery guard
who is helping
Kentucky
defend its title
in basketball

Ralph
Beard
#12

JOE LOUIS, STAY RETIRED! Appeal to a Fading Champion, by JIMMY CANNON

Ralph Beard, a star guard who helped Kentucky win three titles in the 1940s.

quick guard Bob Cousy to just five points. In the final against Baylor, Groza and Beard were the stars. They combined to score 26 points in a 58–42 victory.

Kentucky cruised to the championship again in 1949. This time, the Wildcats beat Oklahoma A&M (now known as Oklahoma State) in the final, 46–36. Kentucky was in control the whole way. In fact, Groza missed 13 minutes of the second half because he was in foul trouble—and he still finished as the game's top scorer!

A new cast of players led the Wildcats to victory in 1951. Cliff Hagan and Frank Ramsey topped a team of excellent shooters. Bill Spivey, a seven-foot center, ruled the backboards. The Wildcats won a thrilling semifinal against Illinois. In the final, they made a great second-half **comeback** against Kansas State. Spivey scored 22 points and had 21 rebounds in a 68–58 victory.

Kentucky's 1957–58 squad was called the "Fiddlin' Five." The team often "fiddled around" and fell behind in games, only to win in the final minutes. The Wildcats lost six times during the season, but Rupp whipped his players into shape for the NCAA Tournament. Forward Johnny Cox and guard Vern Hatton starred against Temple in the semifinals, and then against All-American Elgin Baylor and Seattle in the championship game. The Wildcats held Baylor in check and pulled out an 84–72 victory.

Twenty years passed before the Wildcats celebrated another national championship. In 1977–78, Joe B. Hall coached the Wildcats to a 30–2 record. The team was led by guard Kyle Macy, center Rick Robey, and forward Jack Givens. Their experience was critical in the final over

Basketball
The NCAA Tournament

a young team from Duke. Givens spotted an open area in Duke's **zone defense** and scored 16 points late in the first half. The Blue Devils never recovered, and Kentucky won easily, 94–88.

Coach Rick Pitino led a rebuilding effort in Kentucky during the 1990s. The Wildcats went to the NCAA championship game each year from 1996 to 1998. Pitino had several top players, including forwards Antoine Walker and Ron Mercer, and guard Tony Delk. But it was the depth of the Wildcats that helped them win close games. In 1996, Kentucky defeated Syracuse for the national championship, 76–67. It was a close game until the very end. Delk was the star with seven **3-pointers**.

In the 1997 title game, Kentucky lost to Arizona in **overtime**. Many fans believed the Wildcats would have won if their best shooter, Derek Anderson, had not been out with a knee injury. A year later, the

Wildcats clawed their way back to another championship, this time against Utah. Tubby Smith had helped Pitino rebuild Kentucky's basketball program. In 1997–98, he became the team's coach and took the championship in his first season.

The Wildcats were not expected to win. Their best players had graduated or left for the NBA. However, the "leftovers" had learned well during their years on the bench. Wayne Turner, Jeff Sheppard, Nazr Mohammed, and Scott Padgett led Kentucky to victory over Arizona, 78–69. The Wildcats made baskets under pressure and blocked a record 48 shots during the tournament.

LEFT: Jack Givens scores two of his 41 points against Duke.
ABOVE: Rick Pitino gives instructions to his team during the 1996 NCAA Tournament.

Go-To Guys

FRANK RAMSEY   6′ 3″ Guard/Forward

• BORN: 7/13/1931   • PLAYED FOR VARSITY: 1950–51 TO 1953–54

Frank Ramsey was a good scorer and defender—and a *remarkable* rebounder for his size. He never slowed down and never seemed to get tired. Ramsey was named First-Team **All-SEC** three times.

COTTON NASH   6′ 5″ Forward/Center

• BORN: 7/24/1942   • PLAYED FOR VARSITY: 1961–62 TO 1963–64

Cotton Nash was an amazing athlete. He got his nickname from his white-blond hair. Like Frank Ramsey, he was a valuable scorer and rebounder—and a three-time member of the All-SEC First Team. After college, Nash played pro basketball and pro baseball.

KEVIN GREVEY   6′ 5″ Guard/Forward

• BORN: 5/12/1953   • PLAYED FOR VARSITY: 1972–73 TO 1974–75

Kevin Grevey could score from the inside and the outside. He became the school's first star after Adolph Rupp retired. Grevey was SEC Player of the Year as a sophomore and again as a senior—when he led the Wildcats to the NCAA championship game.

KENNY WALKER   6′ 8″ Forward

- BORN: 8/18/1964   • PLAYED FOR VARSITY: 1982–83 TO 1985–86

Kenny "Sky" Walker was a tremendous leaper. He led the Wildcats to the **Final Four** as a sophomore and was named SEC Player of the Year as a junior and as a senior. Walker once shot a perfect 11-for-11 in an NCAA Tournament game.

TONY DELK   6′ 1″ Guard

- BORN: 1/28/1974
- PLAYED FOR VARSITY: 1992–93 TO 1995–96

When Tony Delk got hot, no one could stop him. He could score from anywhere on the court. Delk was the SEC Player of the Year in 1995–96 and was also named **Most Outstanding Player (MOP)** of the NCAA Tournament that season.

TAYSHAUN PRINCE 6′ 9″ Forward

- BORN: 2/28/1980
- PLAYED FOR VARSITY: 1998–99 TO 2001–02

Tayshaun Prince was Kentucky's best **all-around** player in the first years of the 21st century. He could shoot, rebound, pass, and play defense. In 2001, Prince was named the SEC Player of the Year and the SEC Tournament **Most Valuable Player (MVP)**.

1993-94 University of Kentucky Wildcats

Tony Delk

SUPER SCORERS

These Wildcats were hard to stop when they shot the basketball.

ALEX GROZA   6′ 7″ Center

- BORN: 10/7/1926   • DIED: 1/21/1995
- PLAYED FOR VARSITY: 1944–45 TO 1948–49

Alex Groza was one of the most *agile* big men in college basketball. He was a good passer and rebounder, and no one could stop his sweeping hook shot. He was one of the first college players to average 20 points a game for an entire season. Groza was the top scorer—and MOP—in the 1948 and 1949 NCAA Tournaments.

CLIFF HAGAN   6′ 4″ Center

- BORN: 12/9/1931
- PLAYED FOR VARSITY: 1950–51 TO 1953–54

Cliff Hagan's hook shot was even better than Alex Groza's. He averaged more than 20 points a game twice and was an All-American in both of those seasons. Hagan returned to the university as *athletic director* during the 1970s and 1980s.

DAN ISSEL   6′ 8″ Center

- BORN: 10/25/1948   • PLAYED FOR VARSITY: 1967–68 TO 1969–70

Dan Issel averaged 25 points a game as a Wildcat. As a senior, he broke Cliff Hagan's school record of 51 points in a game when he scored 53 against Mississippi. Issel could make baskets from the outside and also had excellent inside moves.

JACK GIVENS   6′ 4″ Forward

• BORN: 9/21/1956 • PLAYED FOR VARSITY: 1974–75 TO 1977–78

Jack Givens played high school basketball in Lexington. When it came time to pick a college, Kentucky was an easy choice. Givens was a good mid-range shooter. He proved this in the 1978 NCAA title game when he made 18 of 27 shots for 41 points.

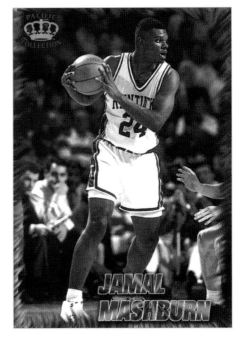

JAMAL MASHBURN   6′ 8″ Forward

• BORN: 11/29/1972

• PLAYED FOR VARSITY: 1990–91 TO 1992–93

Jamal Mashburn was Kentucky's top scorer in his final two seasons with the team. "Mash" was a good outside shooter who could also drive to the basket for monster dunks. He brought a New York in-your-face attitude to Lexington and helped the Wildcats rebuild their program.

ANTOINE WALKER   6′ 8″ Forward

• BORN: 8/12/1976 • PLAYED FOR VARSITY: 1994–95 TO 1995–96

Antoine Walker was a teenager when he wore a Wildcats uniform, but he played like a **veteran**. He was the second-leading scorer on Kentucky's 1996 team. A year earlier, Walker was named the SEC Tournament MVP as a freshman. He led the Wildcats with 23 points in their thrilling overtime victory over Arkansas in the SEC title game.

LEFT: Alex Groza   **ABOVE**: Jamal Mashburn

GAME CHANGERS

These Wildcats had a special talent for controlling the flow of a game.

RALPH BEARD   5′ 10″ Guard

- BORN: 12/2/1927 • DIED: 11/29/2007
  PLAYED FOR VARSITY: 1945–46 TO 1948–49

Ralph Beard led the Wildcats to an NIT title and two NCAA championships. The lightning-quick guard made great plays on offense and defense. Beard was the school's first player to earn All-SEC honors four times.

PAT RILEY   6′ 4″ Forward

- BORN: 3/20/1945 • PLAYED FOR VARSITY: 1964–65 TO 1966–67

Pat Riley and his roommate Louie Dampier formed an unstoppable one-two punch for Kentucky. Riley was a good inside player, while Dampier was a fine outside shooter. Riley led the Wildcats all the way to the NCAA title game in 1966.

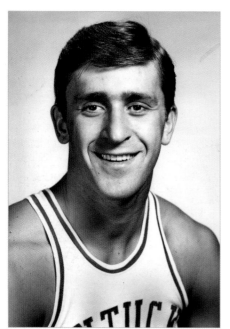

KYLE MACY   6′ 3″ Guard

- BORN: 4/9/1957

- PLAYED FOR VARSITY: 1977–78 TO 1979–80

When Kyle Macy shot free throws with the game on the line, Kentucky fans could breathe easy. No one was better under pressure. In Macy's first year at Kentucky, he led the Wildcats to the NCAA championship.

SAM BOWIE 7′ 1″ Center

• Born: 3/17/1961 • Played for Varsity: 1979–80 to 1983–84

Sam Bowie missed two seasons because of injuries. When he was healthy, no one could handle him. Bowie was a strong, smooth player. When opponents tried to choke off Kentucky's offense, Bowie was the team's "safety valve." He could dribble and pass well enough to break any **full-court press**.

SCOTT PADGETT 6′ 9″ Forward

• Born: 4/19/1976 • Played for Varsity: 1994–95 & 1996–97 to 1998–99

Scott Padgett gave the Wildcats good defense and rebounding. He also had a soft touch on his outside shot. When teams left him open, he burned them for easy baskets. Padgett was at his best in tournament play. He made the All-Final Four team as a sophomore and junior, and was the SEC Tournament MVP as a senior.

RAJON RONDO 6′ 1″ Guard

• Born: 2/22/1986

• Played for Varsity: 2004–05 to 2005–06

When the Wildcats needed a game-winning basket, they put the ball in Rajon Rondo's hands. Rondo's talent for making the "big play" helped him set a school record with 87 steals in a season. He also set a record for rebounds in a game by a guard with 19.

LEFT: Pat Riley   **RIGHT**: Rajon Rondo

On the Sidelines

Adolph Rupp coached the Wildcats for more than 40 years. But he's not the only great coach in school history. Some of the finest minds in basketball have led the Wildcats into battle. One of the first was John Mauer. He was a brilliant coach who drilled his players in the *fundamentals* of the game during the 1920s.

When Rupp replaced Mauer in 1930, he brought a different attitude to the team. Rupp—who learned how to coach basketball from the game's inventor, Dr. James Naismith—was an *intense* competitor who pushed his players to the limits of their ability. He was known as the "Man in the Brown Suit." He always dressed in brown for games. Rupp retired with 876 victories, was named the National Coach of the Year four times, and set school marks of 20 NCAA Tournament appearances and 27 SEC titles.

Many excellent coaches followed Rupp. Joe B. Hall, Eddie Sutton, Rick Pitino, and Tubby Smith all found ways to make the Wildcats a championship team. Hall and Sutton could be strict just like Rupp. Pitino introduced a fast-paced offense to Kentucky and encouraged his players to take 3-point shots. Smith asked his players to work hard on defense and share the ball on offense.

Tubby Smith celebrates by cutting down the net after Kentucky's 1998 national championship.

Rivals

Louisville is Kentucky's natural *rival*. Kentucky and Louisville are the two largest schools in the state, and both often compete for the national championship. The schools battle every year to recruit the best local basketball talent.

The Wildcats square off against the Cardinals once a year. Their annual game is usually played around Christmas vacation. Because Kentucky is known as the "Bluegrass State," the contest is nicknamed the "Battle for the Bluegrass."

What many of today's fans may not realize is that for a very long time, the Wildcats and Cardinals chose not to play each other on the basketball court. From 1923 to 1983, the only time they met was during the NCAA Tournament. That changed after an electrifying overtime battle in 1983. Louisville won the game and advanced to the Final Four. After that, both schools decided that their fans deserved to see an annual clash.

In the years since, the schools have met more than two dozen times. Kentucky has won more often than it has lost. Even so, there always seems to be a new wrinkle to the rivalry. The latest came in 2001, when Louisville coach Denny Crum retired. His replacement

Patrick Sparks sinks one of his three free throws to beat Louisville.

was Rick Pitino—the former Kentucky coach! Pitino is also close friends with John Calipari, the coach that Kentucky hired in 2009. This added even more excitement to the rivalry.

One of the best games in recent years took place early in the 2004–05 season. Louisville shut down the Wildcats in the first half and led 32–16 at halftime. Kentucky came storming back. Patrick Sparks scored 15 points in the last eight minutes. He swished three free throws with one second left to give the Wildcats a *dramatic* 60–58 victory.

One Great Day

During the NCAA Tournament, there is no room for mistakes. The top players and coaches in the country are all competing for the same prize. When a team falls behind in a game, it normally has two chances of coming back—slim and none.

Someone must have forgotten to remind the Wildcats of this in 1998, because they made two incredible comebacks to earn a spot in the championship game. Against Duke, Kentucky trailed by 17 points midway through the second half. The Wildcats fought back and celebrated an 86–84 victory. Days later, in the semifinal game against Stanford, they trailed by double digits. Again, Kentucky made a furious comeback and won another heart-stopper, 86–85.

In the championship game against Utah, the Wildcats found themselves in a familiar position. As they ran off the court at halftime, they were down 41–31. The Utes brimmed with confidence when the second half began. No team had ever lost the championship with such a big lead. When Utah stole the ball and Nazr Mohammed was called for **goaltending**, the Wildcats fell behind by a dozen points.

Jeff Sheppard rises high for a shot attempt against Utah. His basket late in the game put Kentucky ahead for good.

Slowly but surely, they clawed their way back. The Wildcats fought for every rebound and loose ball. In the final minutes, they were full of energy, while the Utes looked exhausted. Jeff Sheppard hit a short jump shot to give Kentucky a 65–64 edge. Utah fouled the Wildcats, hoping they would miss their free throws. But on this night, Kentucky was nearly perfect.

When the final buzzer sounded, the scoreboard said it all: Kentucky 78, Utah 69. Forever after, this group of overachievers would be known as—what else?—the Comeback Cats!

It Really Happened

The 1953–54 Wildcats might have been the finest team Adolph Rupp ever coached. Kentucky finished with a perfect 25–0 record after beating Louisiana State (LSU) in a playoff to become SEC champions. That guaranteed the Wildcats a spot in the NCAA Tournament.

No one doubted that Kentucky was the top team in the country. There was just one problem. One year earlier, the Wildcats did not play basketball at all. They were shut down for a season as punishment for a violation of NCAA rules. Three of the seniors on that team decided to stay in school one more year so they could play a final season. All three—Cliff Hagan, Frank Ramsey, and Lou Tsioropoulos—were named to the All-SEC team.

Before the NCAA Tournament started in 1954, Rupp was told that his three best players would not be allowed to take the court. As far as the NCAA was concerned, Hagan, Ramsey, and Tsioropoulos had already graduated! That made them ineligible to play.

Kentucky fans were crushed. Many thought the Wildcats were good enough to win the national championship. The team still had a talented roster, including Gayle Rose, Billy Evans, Jerry Bird, and

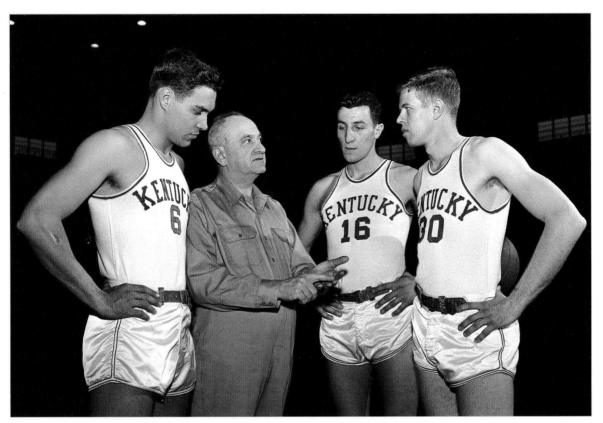

Cliff Hagan, Lou Tsioropoulos, and Frank Ramsey get advice from Adolph Rupp.

Phil Grawemeyer. The players urged Rupp to enter the tournament. But the coach decided not to. Forever after, the 1953–54 Wildcats were known as the best team that never got a taste of "March Madness."

How good were they? According to Rupp, the 1953–54 squad was "the best team we've ever had at Kentucky—and the finest team I have ever seen." He may have been right. That year, the Wildcats outscored their opponents by an average of 27 points. That was an amazing number. Back then, a team was lucky to make one out of three shots. In the years since, only two other teams have won by larger amounts.

Team Spirit

Kentucky's most popular tradition began in 1982. That year, coach Joe B. Hall wanted to get his season off to a great start. The rules stated that teams could not begin practicing until October 15th. Hall announced that the Wildcats would hit the floor at the stroke of midnight. Today, that tradition is called "Big Blue Madness." Fans love it. In 1996, one camped out for 38 days to make sure he was the first in line for a ticket to Big Blue Madness!

Two men who had the same kind of team spirit were Cawood Ledford and Bill Keightley. Both died after long careers with the Wildcats. Ledford was Kentucky's radio broadcaster for more than 40 years. The team named its court after him. Keightley was Kentucky's beloved equipment manager. Everyone knew him as "Mr. Wildcat." The chair that he used during games remains in its same spot, and no one ever sits in it.

Fans also show their support during games. The Wildcats have two mascots. One is a wildcat in a Kentucky jersey. He has been roaming the stands and sidelines since the 1970s. The other is named Scratch. Kentucky's cheerleaders also get the crowd pumped up. When they spell out KENTUCKY during their halftime routine, the Y is often saved for a visiting celebrity.

Actress Ashley Judd cheers on the Wildcats. During a 2004 game, she was chosen to be the Y in KENTUCKY.

Timeline

The basketball season is played from October through March. That means each season takes place at the end of one year and the beginning of the next. In this timeline, the accomplishments of the team are shown by season.

1930–31
Adolph Rupp is hired as coach.

1951–52
Kentucky wins its ninth SEC title in a row.

1957–58
Kentucky wins its fourth NCAA title.

1902–03
Kentucky goes 1–2 in its first season.

1947–48
Kentucky's "Fabulous Five" win the NCAA title and the gold medal in the Olympics.

1969–70
Dan Issel averages 33.9 points per game as a senior.

Adolph Rupp and Johnny Cox show off Kentucky's fourth NCAA trophy.

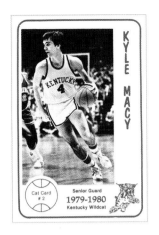

Kyle
Macy

Antoine
Walker

1979–80

Kyle Macy leads the SEC in free throw shooting for the third year in a row.

1994–95

Antoine Walker is named SEC Tournament MVP.

1997–98

Tubby Smith wins the NCAA title in his first year as coach.

1977–78

Jack Givens scores 41 points in the NCAA championship game.

1985–86

Eddie Sutton is named Coach of the Year.

2009–10

John Calipari becomes Kentucky's 22nd coach.

John
Calipari

37

Fun Facts

PRINCE AMONG MEN

In a 2001 game against North Carolina, Tayshaun Prince nailed five 3-pointers to score Kentucky's first 15 points. The Tar Heels never recovered, and the Wildcats won 79–59.

SURVIVOR MAN

Cliff Barker's defense helped Kentucky win the national championship in 1948. A few years before that, Barker was a prisoner of war in Germany. He was part of a bomber crew that was shot down during World War II.

NEVER SAY DIE

In 1994, Kentucky trailed LSU by 31 points with 15 minutes left in the game. The Wildcats made an amazing comeback to win 99–95. Fans call the game the "Mardi Gras Miracle."

FAST COMPANY

Joe B. Hall was a player for Kentucky's 1949 championship team. He also coached the Wildcats to the national title in 1978. Only two others have played for and coached an NCAA champion—basketball legends Bobby Knight and Dean Smith.

TOP CAT

Rick Robey is the only Wildcat to win championships at three different levels. He won a state high school title in 1974, an NCAA title in 1978, and an NBA title in 1981.

SIX PACK

In a 1945 game against Arkansas State, the Wildcats allowed only six points. It is still the greatest defensive game in NCAA history.

SMALL WONDERS

Kentucky's 1965–66 team did not have a starting player taller than 6′ 5″. Even so, they made it all the way to the NCAA championship game. Fans called this team "Rupp's Runts."

LEFT: Tayshaun Prince   **ABOVE**: Joe B. Hall

For the Record

T he great Wildcats teams and players have left their marks on the record books. These are the "best of the best" …

WILDCATS AWARD WINNERS

NCAA TOURNAMENT MOST OUTSTANDING PLAYER		SEC PLAYER OF THE YEAR	
Alex Groza	1947–48	Pat Riley*	1965–66
Alex Groza	1948–49	Tom Parker*	1971–72
Bill Spivey	1950–51	Kevin Grevey*	1972–73
Jack Givens	1977–78	Kevin Grevey*	1974–75
Tony Delk	1995–96	Kyle Macy	1979–80
Jeff Sheppard	1997–98	Kenny Walker	1984–85
		Kenny Walker	1985–86
COACH OF THE YEAR		Jamal Mashburn*	1992–93
Adolph Rupp	1958–59	Tony Delk	1995–96
Adolph Rupp	1965–66	Ron Mercer	1996–97
Eddie Sutton	1985–86	Tayshaun Prince	2000–01
Tubby Smith	2002–03	Keith Bogans*	2002–03
Tubby Smith	2004–05		

Shared this honor with another player.

The 1949 national champs

WILDCATS ACHIEVEMENTS

ACHIEVEMENT	YEAR
National Champions*	1932–33
NIT Champions	1945–46
NIT Finalists	1946–47
NCAA Champions	1947–48
NIT Finalists	1948–49
NCAA Champions	1948–49
NCAA Champions	1950–51
NCAA Champions	1957–58
NCAA Finalists	1965–66
NCAA Finalists	1974–75
NIT Champions	1975–76
NCAA Champions	1977–78
NCAA Champions	1995–96
NCAA Finalists	1996–97
NCAA Champions	1997–98

No tournament held—named champions by Helms Foundation.

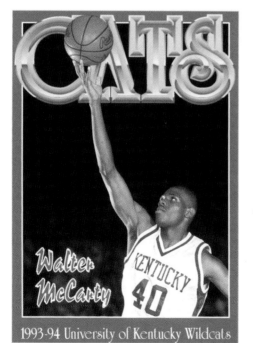

TOP: Bill Spivey, a star for the 1951 national champs. **ABOVE**: Tubby Smith, the coach of the 1998 national champs. **LEFT**: Walter McCarty, a key member of the 1996 national champs.

41

The SEC

T he University of Kentucky is a member of the Southeastern Conference. The SEC was formed in 1932. There are 12 teams in the SEC. Kentucky plays in the Eastern Division of the SEC. These are Kentucky's neighbors …

THE SOUTHEASTERN CONFERENCE

EASTERN DIVISION

1 University of Florida Gators
Gainesville, Florida

2 University of Georgia Bulldogs
Athens, Georgia

3 University of Kentucky Wildcats
Lexington, Kentucky

4 University of South Carolina Gamecocks
Columbia, South Carolina

5 University of Tennessee Volunteers
Knoxville, Tennessee

6 Vanderbilt University Commodores
Nashville, Tennessee

WESTERN DIVISION

7 University of Alabama Crimson Tide
Tuscaloosa, Alabama

8 University of Arkansas Razorbacks
Fayetteville, Arkansas

9 Auburn University Tigers
Auburn, Alabama

10 Louisiana State University Tigers
Baton Rouge, Louisiana

11 University of Mississippi Rebels
Oxford, Mississippi

12 Mississippi State University Bulldogs
Starkville, Mississippi

The College Game

ollege basketball may look like the same game you see professional teams play, but there are some important differences. The first is that college teams play half as many games as the pros do. That's because the players have to attend classes, write papers, and study for exams! Below are several other differences between college and pro basketball.

CLASS NOTES

Most college players are younger than pro players. They are student-athletes who have graduated from high school and now play on their school's varsity team, which is the highest level of competition. Most are between the ages of 18 and 22.

College players are allowed to compete for four seasons. Each year is given a different name or "class"—freshman (first year), sophomore (second year), junior (third year), and senior (fourth year). Sometimes highly skilled players leave college before graduation to play in the pros.

RULE BOOK

There are several differences between the rules in college basketball and the NBA. Here are the most important ones: 1) In college, games last 40 minutes. Teams play two 20-minute halves. In the pros, teams play 48-minute games, divided into four 12-minute quarters. 2) In college, players are disqualified after five personal fouls. In the pros, that number is six. 3) In college, the 3-point line is 20′ 9″ from the basket. In the pros, the line is three feet farther away.

WHO'S NUMBER 1?

How is the national championship of basketball decided? At the end of each season, the top teams are invited to play in the NCAA Tournament. The teams are divided into four groups, and the winner of each group advances to the Final Four. The Final Four consists of two semifinal games. The winners then play for the championship of college basketball.

CONFERENCE CALL

College basketball teams are members of athletic conferences. Each conference represents a different part of the country. For example, the Atlantic Coast Conference is made up of teams from up and down the East Coast. Teams that belong to the same conference usually play each other twice—once on each school's home court. Teams also play games outside their conference. Wins and losses in these games do not count in the conference standings. However, they are very important to a team's national ranking.

TOURNAMENT TIME

At the end of the year, most conferences hold a championship tournament. A team can have a poor record and still be invited to play in the NCAA Tournament if it wins the conference tournament. For many schools, this is an exciting "second chance." In most cases, the regular-season winner and conference tournament winner are given spots in the national tournament. The rest of the tournament "bids" are given to the best remaining teams.

Glossary

3-POINTERS—Baskets made from behind the 3-point line.

ALL-AMERICAN—A college player voted as the best at his position.

ALL-AROUND—Good at all parts of the game.

ALL-SEC—An honor given each year to the conference's best players at each position.

FINAL FOUR—The term for the last four teams remaining in the NCAA Tournament.

FULL-COURT PRESS—A defensive game plan in which a team pressures the opponent for the entire length of the court.

GOALTENDING—A rules violation in which a player blocks a shot on its way down toward the basket or touches a ball on its way through the rim.

LINEUP—The list of players who are playing in a game.

MOST OUTSTANDING PLAYER (MOP)—The award given each year to the best player in the NCAA Tournament.

MOST VALUABLE PLAYER (MVP)—The award given each year to the best player in a conference or in a conference tournament.

NATIONAL BASKETBALL ASSOCIATION (NBA)—The league that has been operating since 1946–47.

NATIONAL COLLEGIATE ATHLETIC ASSOCIATION (NCAA)—The organization that oversees the majority of college sports.

NATIONAL INVITATION TOURNAMENT (NIT)—The competition that is used to determine the champion of college basketball. The NIT began in 1938. Today, there is a preseason and postseason NIT.

NCAA TOURNAMENT—The competition that determines the champion of college basketball.

OVERTIME—The extra period played when a game is tied after 40 minutes.

PROFESSIONAL—A player or team that plays a sport for money. College players are not paid, so they are considered amateurs.

RECRUITED—Offered an athletic scholarship to a prospective student. College teams compete for the best high school players every year.

SEED—The spot awarded to a team in the NCAA Tournament.

SOUTHEASTERN CONFERENCE (SEC)—The league for schools in South Carolina, Georgia, Florida, Alabama, Mississippi, Louisiana, Arkansas, Kentucky, and Tennessee. The SEC played its first season in 1933.

VETERAN—A player with great experience.

ZONE DEFENSE—A defense in which players are responsible for guarding an area of the court rather than covering a specific offensive player.

OTHER WORDS TO KNOW

AGILE—Quick and graceful.

ATHLETIC DIRECTOR—The person in charge of a college's sports program.

CAMPUS—The grounds and buildings of a college.

COMEBACK—The process of catching up from behind, or making up a large deficit.

DECADE—A period of 10 years; also specific periods, such as the 1950s.

DRAMATIC—Sudden or surprising.

ERAS—Periods of time in history.

FEROCIOUS—Extremely intense or frightening.

FUNDAMENTALS—The most basic parts of something.

INTENSE—Very strong or very deep.

LOGO—A symbol or design that represents a company or team.

OLYMPICS—An international sports competition held every four years.

REMARKABLE—Unusual or exceptional.

RIVAL—Extremely emotional competitor.

SATIN—A smooth, shiny fabric.

STRATEGY—A plan or method for succeeding.

SUFFOCATING—High energy and pressure filled.

SYNTHETIC—Made in a laboratory, not in nature.

TRADITION—A belief or custom that is handed down from generation to generation.

Places to Go

ON THE ROAD

KENTUCKY WILDCATS
430 West Vine Street
Lexington, Kentucky 40507
(859) 257-1916

NAISMITH MEMORIAL BASKETBALL HALL OF FAME
1000 West Columbus Avenue
Springfield, Massachusetts 01105
(877) 4HOOPLA

ON THE WEB

THE KENTUCKY WILDCATS   www.ukathletics.com
  * *Learn more about the Wildcats*

SOUTHEASTERN CONFERENCE   www.secsports.com
  * *Learn more about the Southeastern Conference teams*

THE BASKETBALL HALL OF FAME   www.hoophall.com
  * *Learn more about history's greatest players*

ON THE BOOKSHELF

To learn more about the sport of basketball, look for these books at your library or bookstore:
  * Stewart, Mark and Kennedy, Mike. *Swish: the Quest for Basketball's Perfect Shot.* Minneapolis, Minnesota: Millbrook Press, 2009.
  * Ramen, Fred. *Basketball: Rules, Tips, Strategy & Safety.* New York, New York: Rosen Central, 2007.
  * Labrecque, Ellen. *Basketball.* Ann Arbor, Michigan: Cherry Lake Publishing, 2009.

Index

PAGE NUMBERS IN **BOLD** REFER TO ILLUSTRATIONS.

Anderson, Derek 18
Azubuike, Kelenna 11
Barker, Cliff 16, 38
Baylor, Elgin 17
Beard, Ralph 7, 16, **16**, 17, 24
Bird, Jerry 7, 32
Bogans, Keith 11, 40
Bowie, Sam 9, **9**, 25
Buchheit, George 6
Calipari, John 29, 37, **37**
Calverley, Ernie 16
Chapman, Rex 9
Cousy, Bob 17
Cox, Johnny 7, 17, **36**
Crum, Denny 28
Dampier, Louie 7, 24
Delk, Tony 9, 18, 21, **21**, 40
Epps, Anthony **4**
Evans, Billy 32
Givens, Jack 7, 18, **18**, 23, 37, 40
Grawemeyer, Phil 33
Grevey, Kevin 7, 20, 40
Groza, Alex 7, 16, 17, 22, **22**, 40
Hagan, Cliff 7, **14**, 17, 22, 32, **33**
Hall, Joe B. 7, 18, 27, 35, 39, **39**
Hatton, Vern 17
Hayden, Basil 6
Issel, Dan 7, **7**, 22, 36
Jones, Wallace "Wah Wah" 16
Judd, Ashley **34**
Keightley, Bill 35
Knight, Bobby 39
Ledford, Cawood 35
Macy, Kyle 7, 18, 24, 37, **37**, 40
Magloire, Jamaal 11

Mashburn, Jamal 23, **23**, 40
Mauer, John 27
McCarty, Walter 9, **41**
Meeks, Jodie 11, **15**
Mercer, Ron **4**, **8**, 9, 18, 40
Mohammed, Nazr 19, 30
Morris, Randolph 11
Naismith, Dr. James 27
Nash, Cotton 7, 20
Padgett, Scott 19, 25
Parker, Tom 40
Pitino, Rick 9, 18, 19, **19**, 27, 29
Prince, Tayshaun 11, 21, 38, **38**, 40
Ramsey, Frank 7, 17, 20, 32, **33**
Riley, Pat 7, 24, **24**, 40
Robey, Rick 7, 18, 39
Rollins, Kenny 16
Rondo, Rajon 11, 25, **25**
Rose, Gayle 32
Rupp, Adolph 6, **6**, 7, 13, 17, 20,
.... 27, 32, 33, **33**, 36, **36**, 40
Sheppard, Jeff 19, 31, **31**, 40
Smith, Adrian 7
Smith, Dean 39
Smith, Orlando "Tubby" 9, 11, 19,
.... **26**, 27, 37, 40, **41**
Sparks, Patrick 29, **29**
Spivey, Bill 17, 40, **41**
Sutton, Eddie 27, 37, 40
Tsioropoulos, Lou 32, **33**
Turner, Wayne 9, 19
Turpin, Mel 9
Walker, Antoine **4**, 9, 18,
.... 23, 37, **37**
Walker, Kenny 9, 21, 40

About the Author

MARK STEWART has written more than 30 books on basketball players and teams, and over 100 sports books for kids. He has also interviewed dozens of athletes, politicians, and celebrities. Although Mark grew up in New York City, as a young fan he discovered Kentucky basketball while watching American Basketball Association games on TV. Dan Issell and Louie Dampier of the Wildcats were early American Basketball Assocation All-Stars. Mark comes from a family of writers. His grandfather was Sunday Editor of *The New York Time*s and his mother was Articles Editor for *Ladies' Home Journal* and *McCall's*. Mark became interested in sports during lazy summer days spent at the Connecticut home of his father's godfather, sportswriter John R. Tunis. Mark is a graduate of Duke University, with a degree in History. He lives with his wife Sarah, and daughters Mariah and Rachel, overlooking Sandy Hook, New Jersey.

MATT ZEYSING is the resident historian at the Basketball Hall of Fame in Springfield, Massachusetts. His research interests include the origins of the game of basketball, the development of professional basketball in the first half of the 20th century, and the culture and meaning of basketball in American society.